SPACEMANATEE!

By KATIE GILSTRAP

Illustrated by ALICE SAMUEL

MAGINATION PRESS · AMERICAN PSYCHOLOGICAL ASSOCIATION · WASHINGTON, D.C.

FOR JACK AND ATTICUS—I LOVE YOU
TO THE MOON AND BACK!— KG

FOR TILLY, MY STAR—AS

Books for Kids From the
American Psychological Association

Magination Press is a registered trademark of the American Psychological Association. Order books at maginationpress.org, or call 1-800-374-2721.

Book design by Rachel Ross

Printed by Lake Book Manufacturing, Inc., Melrose Park, IL

Library of Congress Cataloging-in-Publication Data

Names: Gilstrap, Katie, author. | Samuel, Alice, illustrator.

Title: Spacemanatee! / by Katie Gilstrap; illustrated by Alice Samuel.

Other titles: Space manatee

Description: Washington, DC: Magination Press, [2023] | Summary: Sweet-natured manatee Anna Lee, believing the moon is home to a Magical Manatee Queen, flies to the lunar surface to prove her existence to her friend, the Loon.

Identifiers: LCCN 2022023887 (print) | LCCN 2022023888 (ebook) | ISBN 9781433840371 (hardcover) | ISBN 9781433841309 (ebook)

Subjects: CYAC: Stories in rhyme. | Manatees—Fiction. | Loons—Fiction. | Space flight to the moon—Fiction. | LCGFT: Animal fiction. | Stories in rhyme.

Classification: LCC PZ8.3.G4234 Sp 2023 (print) | LCC PZ8.3.G4234 (ebook) | DDC [E]—dc23

LC record available at https://lccn.loc.gov/2022023887

LC ebook record available at https://lccn.loc.gov/2022023888

Manufactured in the United States of America

10 9 8 7 6 5 4 3 2 1

ANNA LEE MANATEE
LIVES IN THE SEA.
HER BODY IS SLOW,
BUT HER SPIRIT IS FREE!

AT NIGHT, SHE MEETS UP WITH HER GOOD FRIEND, THE LOON.
THEY WADE IN THE WATER AND STARE AT THE MOON.

SQUINTING HER EYES, ANNA SAYS TO THE BIRD,
"THERE'S A MANATEE UP ON THE MOON, SO I'VE HEARD."

THE LOON SHAKES HIS HEAD AND CONTINUES TO STARE.
"THE MOON IS THE MOON. THERE'S NO MANATEE THERE."

WITH A FLIP OF HER LIP, ANNA HUNCHES HER SHOULDERS.
"THE MOON IS WAY MORE THAN JUST CRATERS AND BOULDERS!

IT'S HOME TO A MAGICAL MANATEE QUEEN
WHO TRAVELS THROUGH QUASARS AND GALAXIES GREEN!"

THE LOON FLITS HIS FEATHERS AND ROLLS BACK HIS EYES.
"THEN WHY DON'T YOU GO UP AND PROVE IT?" HE SIGHS.

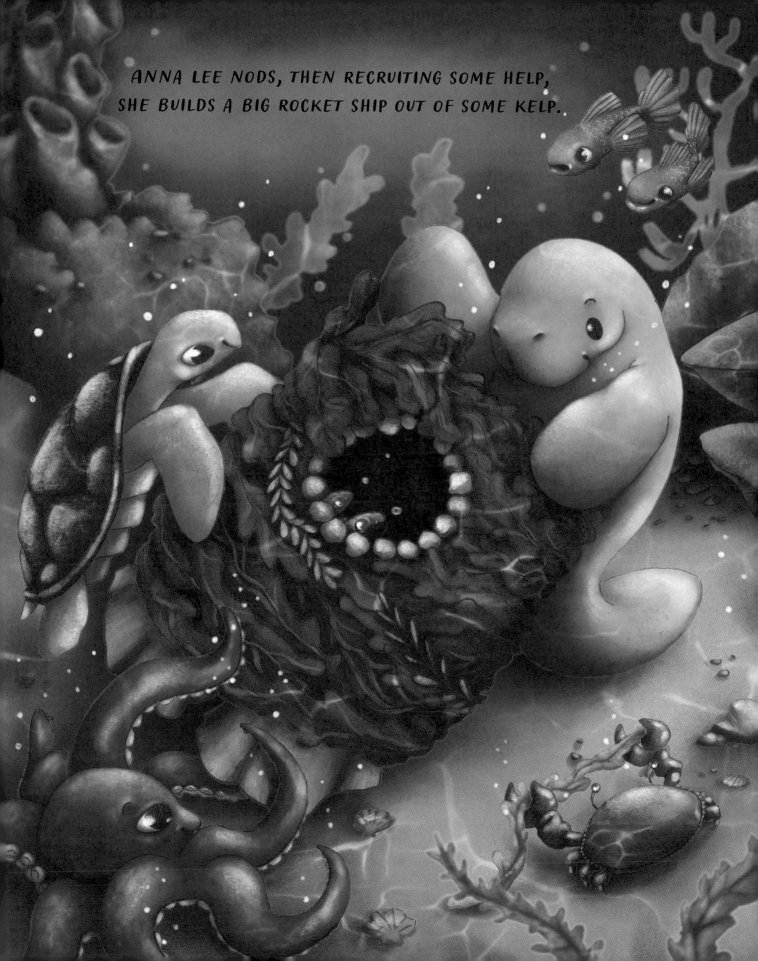

ANNA LEE NODS, THEN RECRUITING SOME HELP,
SHE BUILDS A BIG ROCKET SHIP OUT OF SOME KELP.

SHE THEN MAKES A HELMET OF SEA GLASS AND SHELLS.
THE LOON TILTS HIS HEAD. "SAFETY FIRST!"
ANNA YELLS.

SLOWLY BUT SURELY, SHE WORKS 'TIL SHE'S DONE. THEN CLIMBING ABOARD, SHE COUNTS DOWN:

"THREE!
TWO!
ONE!"

SHAKING, THE ROCKET SHIP SHOOTS THROUGH THE SKY.
ANNA WAVES BACK AT THE LOON AND SHOUTS, "BYE!"

SHE PEERS OUT THE WINDOW. THERE'S SO MUCH TO SEE!
ANNA EXCLAIMS,

"I'M A SPACEMANATEE!"

SHE ZIPS PAST A QUASAR, AND ZOOMING IN FLIGHT,
SHE SINGS THROUGH A SHOWER OF METEOR LIGHTS!

SHE CIRCLES A COMET AND SOARS THROUGH ITS TAILS.
NOW JUST UP AHEAD... "IT'S THE MOON!" ANNA WAILS.

WITH HELMET IN PLACE, SHE BRACES TO LAND.
SHE LOWERS HER ROCKET SHIP INTO THE SAND.

"THE SEA COW HAS LANDED!" SHE YAWPS WITH A YIP.

AND WITH A DEEP BREATH, SHE SLINKS OUT OF HER SHIP.

SHE STEPS TO THE SURFACE AND WHISPER—SHOUTS, "SOON!
I'LL FIND THE MANATEE HERE ON THE MOON!"
FLAPPING HER FLIPPERS, SHE LOOKS ALL AROUND.
SHE CREEPS OVER CRATERS AND ROOTS THROUGH THE GROUND.

SHE VENTURES IN VALLEYS AND POKES AT THE PEAKS
FOR WHAT FEELS LIKE MINUTES. NO, HOURS. NO, WEEKS.
SHE CIRCLES THE MOON COUNTERCLOCKWISE AND BACK.
NO SIGN OF THE SPACE QUEEN. NOT EVEN A TRACK.

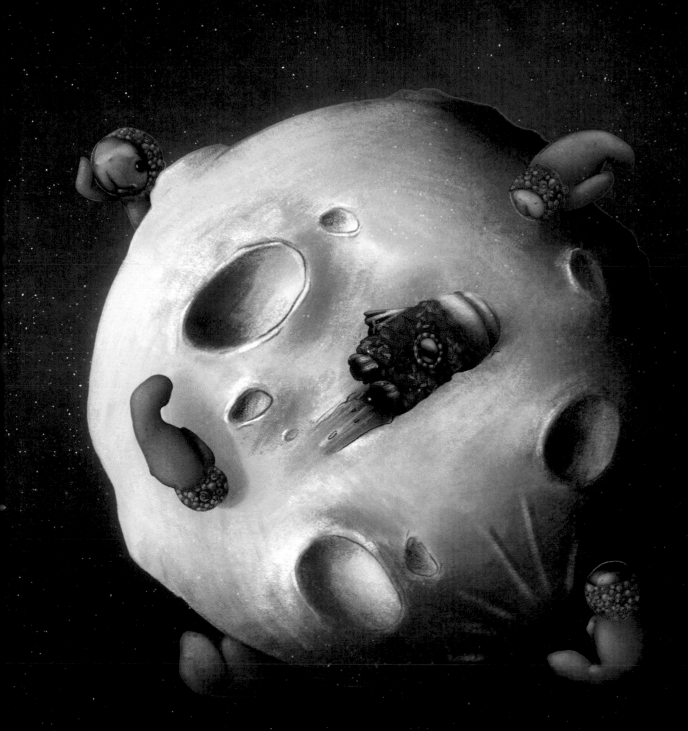

DEFEATED, SHE PLOPS HERSELF DOWN IN A DUNE.
"I GUESS THERE'S NO MANATEE HERE ON THE MOON."

SLOWLY BUT SURELY, SHE ROLLS TO HER HIP,
THEN SADLY, SHE SHIMMIES ON BACK TO THE SHIP.

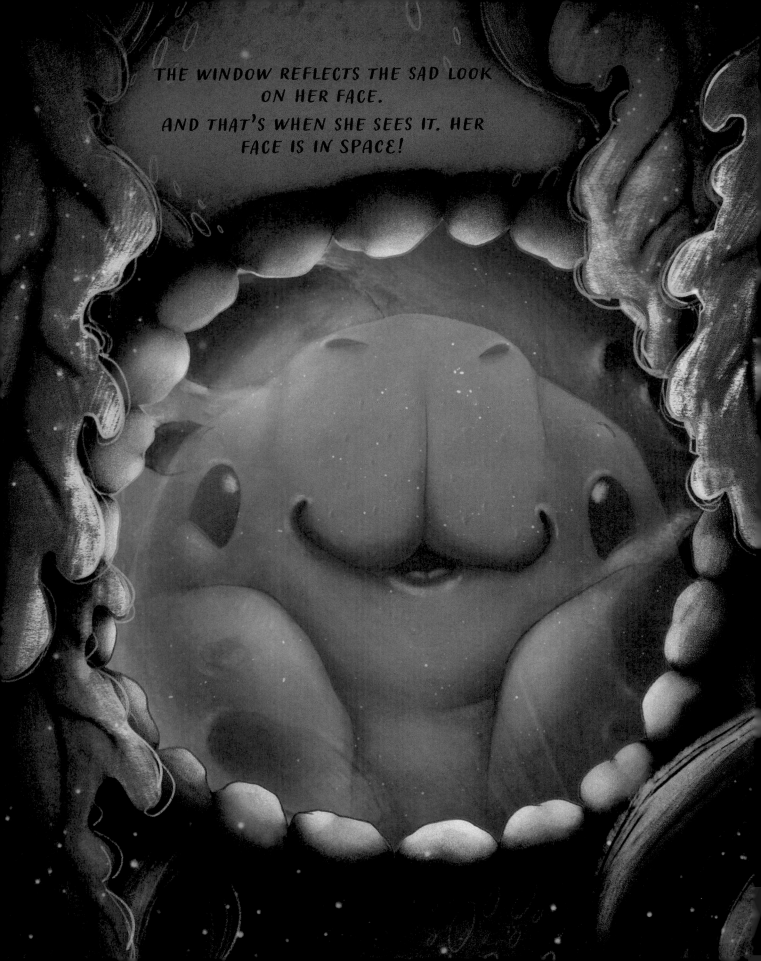

THE WINDOW REFLECTS THE SAD LOOK
ON HER FACE.
AND THAT'S WHEN SHE SEES IT. HER
FACE IS IN SPACE!

ANNA LEE WARBLES AND WOBBLES WITH GLEE:
"THERE'S A MANATEE UP ON THE MOON,
AND IT'S

MΣ!"

ANNA LEE PRESSES HER SNOUT TO THE SAND
AND KISSES THE SPOT WHERE HER FLOPPY LIPS LAND.

SHE LEAVES AN IMPRESSION OF COURAGE AND GRACE.
THE PRINT OF A BONA FIDE MOONATEE FACE!

WHEN ANNA GOES HOME, SHE MEETS UP WITH THE LOON,
AND JUST AFTER TWILIGHT, THEY LOOK AT THE MOON.

SOMETHING THERE CATCHES THE LOON'S BEADY EYE:
IT'S THE MAGICAL MOONATEE UP IN THE SKY!

STARTLED, THE LOON HOPS UP HIGH IN THE AIR.
"I SEE IT! I SEE THERE'S A MANATEE THERE!"

ANNA LEE GRINS AS SHE SINGS WITH A SQUEAL,
"WHAT DID I TELL YOU? I KNEW SHE WAS REAL!"

GLOSSARY OF SKY AND SEA

COMET
Also known as a "dirty snowball," a comet is a cosmic ball of ice, gas, and dust that orbits the Sun. Heat from the Sun turns the ice into dusty vapor trails that cascade behind the comet, giving it the appearance of having a tail.

CRATER
A large, rounded dent on the surface of the moon. Formed by the impact of meteor strikes, there are over 100,000 craters on the moon.

GALAXY
A large group of stars held together by gravity. The Milky Way Galaxy, home to planet Earth, is only one of the 200 billion galaxies in the observable universe.

METEOR
A rocky or metallic chunk of space debris that produces a bright light when it enters the Earth's atmosphere. Also known as a "shooting star," most meteors burn up in the sky before they have a chance to reach the Earth's surface.

QUASAR
An extremely bright and powerful area found in the middle of galaxies containing supermassive black holes. Many scientists believe the radiation that a quasar produces actually powers the black hole in its center.

TWILIGHT
The period of time just before sunrise and after sunset when scattered Sun rays glow softly against an otherwise dark sky.

KELP
A type of large, brown seaweed with a long stalk. Sometimes, kelp will grow into underwater "kelp forests" that serve as homes to many marine animals.

LOON
An aquatic bird distinguishable by its short tail, webbed feet, and unique call. Though loons are clumsy on land, they are exceedingly graceful in the water.

MANATEE
A sizable, slow-moving sea animal that lives in the shallow coastal waters and rivers around the tropical Atlantic. With a mouth full of molars designed to grind sea grass, manatees are the only vegetarian sea mammals on Earth. Sporting flat, round, and powerful tail flippers, they are thought to have inspired the original mermaid legends.

SEA COW
Nickname for any animal in the sirenian group of mammals, including the dugong and the manatee.

SEA GLASS
Naturally weathered pieces of glass which, after tumbling in the ocean's waves for a number of years, look like colorful, polished rocks. Sea glass can be found in a variety of tints, but the most common are green, blue, clear, and brown.

SHELL
The hardened outer layer of a marine mollusk's body. Shells can be smooth or spiky, ridged or rounded, flat or conical, depending on the type of animal living inside. Empty shells found on the beach are from mollusks who no longer need this protective layer.

READER'S NOTE

BY JULIA MARTIN BURCH, PHD

Anna Lee is one confident manatee, but chances are she wasn't born fully confident in herself and her dreams! Children develop a sense of self-confidence through life experiences. These experiences can include mastering new skills, learning to handle challenges, and having the space and support to explore new things. As a parent or caregiver, you have many opportunities to help foster your child's self-confidence and belief in their dreams.

HELP YOUR CHILD LEARN NEW SKILLS

From a young age, teach your child how to take care of themselves, their possessions, and the world around them. Children feel proud, competent, and self-reliant—building blocks of self-confidence—when they know they are capable.

Give your child responsibilities around the house. Even very young children can do small tasks like moving laundry from the washer to the dryer. As your child becomes more confident in their ability to do daily tasks, increase their level of independence and responsibility. When your child inevitably struggles, teach them how to talk themselves through the challenge. It can be helpful to ask them what they would say to a friend who was in a similar position. For example, they might say to themselves, "this is hard, but I'm good at solving problems. I can do it!"

LET THEM GET MESSY

Self-confidence does not develop in a vacuum. Children must struggle, make mistakes, and navigate their own way through challenges with an age-appropriate degree of independence. This powerful cycle helps to instill in children a sense that they can handle future challenges which in turn, increases their self-confidence.

To support this, strive to create a mistake-friendly culture in your family in which all family members are encouraged to take (appropriate) risks in pursuit of their interests and dreams.

When your child struggles or makes mistakes, be there for them emotionally, but resist the well-intended urge to swoop in and protect them from the emotional discomfort. Experiencing small doses of disappointment and sadness gives children an opportunity to practice coping with those emotions and coming out stronger on the other side. It is particularly powerful for the development of self-confidence for a child to know that they handled a problem using their own internal resources.

SUPPORT THEIR MOONATEE DREAMS!

As you know, children tend to have all kinds of wild and wonderful beliefs and dreams—much like a manatee on the moon! Listen curiously and non-judgmentally when your child shares about their interests. Ask open ended questions such as "what excites you about that?" or "what would be the most fun and the hardest things about that?" Resist the urge to share practical advice on how realistic their ideas or passions might be. Instead, strive to share their enthusiasm. Help them think through what they might do to chase their dreams.

When your child pursues new interests, praise their efforts and help them reflect on how it feels to go after their dreams—no matter how it went! For example, you might say "I love how you were willing to try gymnastics even though you have never done it before! How did it feel to try something you have been interested in for so long?" Helping your child reflect on how good it feels to pursue their dreams—even when there are bumps in the road!—helps to instill internal motivation to keep trying.

Julia Martin Burch, PhD, is a clinical psychologist in private practice. She specializes in evidence-based treatments, including cognitive behavior therapy and exposure and response prevention therapy for youth anxiety, obsessive compulsive, and related disorders. She completed her training at Fairleigh Dickinson University and Massachusetts General Hospital/Harvard Medical School.

KATIE GILSTRAP, wildlife advocate and space enthusiast, earned her Master of Arts in English from Kansas State University. Diagnosed with obsessive-compulsive disorder as an adolescent, Katie now strives to celebrate neurodiversity in children's literature by writing kid-friendly books that inspire confidence, courage, and self-acceptance. Though she is now a full-time author, most of her writerly inspiration stems from the years she spent working as a veterinary technician. *Spacemanatee!* is her first book. She currently lives in south central Kansas.

Visit katiegilstrap.com and @byKatieGilstrap on Twitter and Instagram.

ALICE SAMUEL is an illustrator based in Swansea, Wales, who graduated with a BA (Hons) in illustration.

Visit @alicesamuel_illustration on Instagram.

MAGINATION PRESS is the children's book imprint of the American Psychological Association. APA works to advance psychology as a science and profession and as a means of promoting health and human welfare. Magination Press books reach young readers and their parents and caregivers to make navigating life's challenges a little easier. It's the combined power of psychology and literature that makes a Magination Press book special.

Visit maginationpress.org and @MaginationPress on Facebook, Twitter, Instagram, and Pinterest.